D1376096

TO ALL MY OLD
AND NEW FRIENDS
WHO ALWAYS MAKE ME
FEEL AT HOME.

First published 2014 by
Macmillan Children's Books an
imprint of Pan Macmillan
This edition published 2020 by
Macmillan Children's Books
The Smithson, 6 Briset Street, London
EC1M 5NR
www.panmacmillan.com

(PB) ISBN: 978-1-5290-4511-6
(EB) ISBN: 978-1-4472-9283-8

Text and illustrations copyright
© Marta Altés 2014
Thanks to my editor Emily Ford
and designer Sharon King-Chai

All rights reserved. No part of this
publication may be reproduced, stored
in or introduced into a retrieval system,
or transmitted, in any form, or by
any means (electronic, mechanical,
photocopying, recording or otherwise)
without the prior written permission of
the publisher.

1 3 5 7 9 8 6 4 2

A CIP catalogue record for this book is
available from the British Library.

Printed in China

MARTA ALTÉS

MY NEW HOME

MACMILLAN CHILDREN'S BOOKS

We've just moved house

and I feel so far from home.

I was happy in my old house.

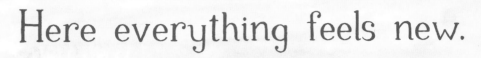

Here everything feels new.

I don't really like it.

New can be scary . . .

. . . and a little bit lonely.

Dad says
not to worry.

He says that
when I least
expect it . . .

I'll find new adventures.

And adventures
make loneliness
disappear . . .

I still miss my old friends.

But sometimes it feels
like they are here.

When I moved house
I felt far from home.

Here everything feels new.

But new can be exciting!

I think I'm very lucky . . .

. . . and I feel at
home again.

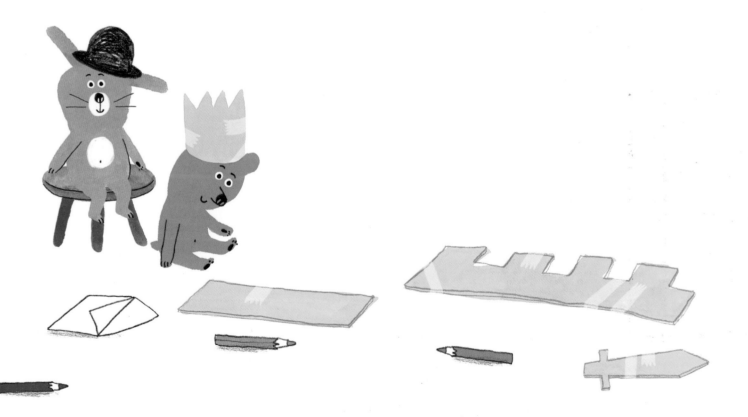